The Day the
Rebels Came
to Town

ROBERT HOUGH

The Day the Rebels Came to Town

Grass Roots Press

First published in 2011 by Grass Roots Press

The Good Reads series is funded in part by the Government of Canada's Office of Literacy and Essential Skills.

Grass Roots Press also gratefully acknowledges the financial support for its publishing programs provided by the following agencies: the Government of Canada through the Canada Book Fund and the Government of Alberta through the Alberta Foundation for the Arts.

Grass Roots Press would also like to thank ABC Life Literacy Canada for their support. Good Reads® is used under licence from ABC Life Literacy Canada.

Library and Archives Canada Cataloguing in Publication

Hough, Robert, 1963–
    The day the rebels came to town / Robert Hough.

(Good reads series)
ISBN 978–1–926583–35–8

    1. Readers for new literates. I. Title. II. Series: Good reads series (Edmonton, Alta.)

PS8565.O7683D39 2011   428.6'2   C2011–902729–1

Printed and bound in Canada.

Distributed to libraries and educational and community organizations by
Grass Roots Press
www.grassrootsbooks.net

Distributed to retail outlets by
HarperCollins Canada Ltd.
www.harpercollins.ca

Chapter One

The year was 1920, and Mexico was at war with itself. Rebels rode through the land in small groups, stealing money, food, and horses to help fight the army. The army did the same, often shooting those who helped the rebels. For those who only wanted peace, it was a time of great sadness and fear.

Carlos Orozco was twenty-eight years old. He worked in the kitchen of his father's café on the square in the centre of town. Mostly, he spent his days cooking eggs, beans, tacos, and stews. The café also served beer, as well as soups made from peppers and corn. Though Carlos's days were long, he knew he was lucky to have any job at all.

One day, as Carlos washed dishes, his father came into the kitchen.

"Carlos," he said. "A group of horsemen is riding in from the south."

"You can hear the drumming of hooves?" asked Carlos.

"Yes," said his father.

Within an hour, about a half-dozen riders entered the town. Looking on, Carlos could tell that they were rebels. They were unwashed, wore huge moustaches, and had bands of bullets crossed over their chests. Still riding their horses, the rebels filled the town's central plaza in front of the café. At the same time, the women of the village slipped out of their back doors. They took shelter in the hills ringing the town.

Soon, the rebels grew hungry and went to the only place in town that served hot food. As they filed into The Orozco Café, the rest of the customers quickly finished their meals. They all left, fearing trouble. The rebels sat and started talking loudly. One man, whom the others called "Captain," yelled for service. He was a large man, and he wore a pair of pistols, one on each side. Both guns were the size of small dogs.

Carlos's father went to greet the rebels.

"Food," ordered the captain. "Lots of it. And beer."

Carlos prepared plate after plate of tacos, rice, beans, and chicken with lime. No matter how hard he worked, his father kept rushing into the kitchen. "Please, Carlos," he said. "Work faster. We can't keep men like these waiting."

After an hour or so, the shouts for food died down. The rebels now shouted for tequila. Carlos's father didn't want to give them strong liquor after all the beer they had drunk, but he had no choice.

Carlos left the kitchen, thinking that his father might need help with clearing the tables. The rebels were all sitting back in their chairs, hands resting on full stomachs, burping.

"Hey," said the captain.

Carlos looked up and saw that the rebel leader was talking to him.

"You the cook?"

"Yes," said Carlos.

"That was good. Damn good. I like the way you cook things here in the South."

The room went silent.

"Thank you," said Carlos.

"We could use someone like you."

Carlos said nothing.

"Yes, yes. Our last cook had a bit of an… of an accident." The men around him snickered. "So I am giving you a job in our Army of the North. You will fight for the freedom of Mexico. You will be under the supreme command of Pancho Villa himself. What do you think of that? We're riding back north today."

"Please," Carlos said. "It is an honour. But I must say no. I am needed here."

The rebel captain walked toward Carlos. He wore spurs, and they jangled as he came near. Dust rose from the floor. When he was less than an arm's length away, he stopped. Carlos could smell the garlic and onion he himself had chopped early that morning. He could also smell the tequila on the man's breath.

"Let me put it this way," said the captain. "If you don't take this job, I'll be forced to think you don't support our cause."

He pulled one of his guns from its holster and grinned. "And I don't need to tell you how we deal with them types."

Chapter Two

The rebel gang travelled north, taking Carlos with them. In each town, they chose one or two more young men to come with them. Some liked the idea of carrying a large gun, in a country without laws, and were pleased to join. Others were like Carlos and wanted no part in the terror spreading across the land. None of this mattered. The captain just took the men he wanted.

At the end of each day, when the sunset turned the sky a blaze of red, they set up camp. Carlos's job started then. Despite having ridden all day, he had to build a fire, set up his grate and stew pot, and cook dinner. Often, Carlos was so tired by the time the meal ended that he would fall asleep on top of his bed roll. He wouldn't even take off the clothes he'd worn all day. In less than a week, he was as bearded and dusty as the other rebels. He felt tired all the time, and his muscles ached. He smelled of horses, gun oil, and sweat. He missed his father and his little village in the hills of the South.

Slowly, the gang made its way toward the northern states. Every day, they rode through a world of cactus, scrubby bushes, rattlesnakes, and scorpions. Vultures often flew above them, as though waiting for them to die in the broiling heat. As the land became drier, the towns grew farther and farther apart. The men became bored and their moods turned foul. Some even began to complain to the captain. They wanted to fight, they wanted women, they wanted a night in a real bed.

Finally, the captain had no choice but to please them. "I know a town near the border," he told them. "It's a little out of our way, but that means no one's beaten us there. And who knows? Could be we might find us some army types, hiding like the dogs they are. Better make sure your pistols are oiled, boys."

When the men heard this, they cheered.

After half a day of hard riding, they pulled into the town of Rosita. It was much smaller than they expected. They saw only a church, some shabby buildings around a small square, and a couple of narrow dirt streets. Some of the men groaned, and others complained again to the captain.

"Looks aren't everything," said the captain. "I know for a fact there's a decent-sized tavern, just over there. And I know one other thing that I been keeping back. As a surprise, sort of."

"What's that?" someone asked.

The captain smiled. "Rosita has one of the best brothels in all of northern Mexico. It'll open up later. Now who's gonna join me for a beer?"

The men cheered and followed the captain into a small building with a sign saying "Fernando" over the door. Carlos did not join them. He had to set up his stew pot and grate in the dusty town square and simmer pinto beans for that night's meal. There was also bread to make, cactus leaves to chop, and corn to husk. At least, thought Carlos, I'll have lots of time to cook.

The sun was so strong that it bleached the sky, turning it the light blue of a faded cotton shirt. The adobe buildings of the town looked faded, too. The sun had taken all the colour out of their mud bricks. As Carlos worked, he kept one eye on the tavern. At first, he could not hear the men. Soon, however, the rebels were laughing, talking loudly, and calling for more liquor. Carlos started his fire and began heating a huge pot of well water. He soon started hearing battle songs, sung loudly and off-key, drifting from the tavern's window and open door.

As the beans cooked, Carlos was pleased to have some time to himself. He sat in the shade of the square's low wall and decided he might enjoy a little nap. His thoughts had just started to soften and turn strange when loud noises awoke him.

The noises came from the tavern: yelling and foul language and the crashing of chairs. Of course, Carlos guessed the problem. The captain had no doubt told the owner that he had just helped the cause by giving the rebels free drinks. Most tavern owners accepted this, knowing the risk of saying no. Some, however, did not.

Then Carlos heard gunfire. Rebels spilled out of the tavern, so drunk they could barely stand. They were all laughing, and a moment later Carlos saw why. Flames began licking out of the window, followed by clouds of thick, black smoke. Then the owner stumbled out the door. He coughed madly while swatting at his flaming left sleeve. Carlos swallowed hard and wished only that his country was at peace.

Just then, Carlos noticed that he was not the only person in the town square. An old, grey-haired man was walking toward the tavern. He wore denim pants and a cowboy hat, and his feet kicked up dust as he walked. A few seconds later, the rebels came into the square, still laughing and swearing and very, very drunk.

"Hey," the old man called in a loud, firm voice. "*You.*"

The rebels went silent and looked over. The captain raised an eyebrow.

"Yes, you," the old man said again. "You will stop this."

The rebels drew their pistols. The captain sneered.

"Jesus Christ," he laughed. "Who in the hell are *you*?"

"I am Roberto Cruz. I am the mayor of Rosita. I am the mayor of this town."

"The mayor! So *you* run this piece of shit town. Well, Mr. Mayor. You got something to say to me?"

"I do."

"Then say it, you old buzzard."

"You will leave. You will pack up your men and you will leave this place. We have nothing to do with this war of yours. This is a peaceful place. You have no reason to be here."

The captain narrowed his eyes and approached the old man.

"We ain't here for the war, old man. We're here for the women."

"You won't find any here. The brothel closed years ago, and all the other women have run away to the desert. You're in a town of men, now."

The captain looked around, noticing for the first time that he had not seen a single woman in the town. His eyes flared with anger, and the rest of his face seemed to darken. He walked around the mayor in slow, tight circles. Suddenly he stopped, struck with an idea.

The captain turned toward Carlos.

"Cook!" he called, an evil grin crossing his face.

Carlos walked toward the captain. His heart pounded and his legs shook, as though too weak to support his body. He could smell wood smoke and sweat coming up from his damp, dirty shirt. He stopped before the captain.

"Yes, sir?" he said.

"Must be a little boring, cooking beans all the time."

As Carlos stood there under the baking sun, he knew he had to agree. "Yes, Chief," he said. "It's very boring."

The captain moved in close. "Ah, well. I have good news for you, then," he said. "I'm going to make you a real soldier. You'd like that? To be a soldier in our Army of the North? Under the supreme command of Pancho Villa? Of course you would. It'd make a man out of you, eh, cook?" As he spoke, he waved one of his pistols.

A flock of crows took flight, briefly forming a shadow above. In that moment, the captain seemed to lose his good cheer. He grabbed Carlos's forearm and put the gun in his hand. He then pointed toward the town's old mayor. For some reason, Carlos noticed that the mayor was wearing a clean blue denim shirt. It was a shirt that someone must have ironed for him that very morning.

"We have arrested this man. He is against the rebel cause. Please take care of him."

Carlos looked into the eyes of the captain. "No, please, I'm just a cook."

"Oh no, you trembling little coward. You are a proud member of the Army of the North. You are under the supreme command of Pancho-god-damn-Villa! Now do your job."

"Please, sir. I am begging…"

"Do it!"

Carlos didn't move. The captain grabbed the hand that held the pistol and raised it. Now the gun's long barrel pointed at the old mayor's face. Carlos began to whimper. He and his friends used to kill crows and give them to their mothers to bake into pies. Apart from those crows, he had never killed anything in his life.

"Please," Carlos pleaded. "Don't force me to do this."

This caused the other rebels to laugh and slap their thighs. One fell to his knees and began to vomit. The captain, however, was very angry. He pulled his other pistol from its holster and put the tip of the barrel to Carlos's head. "It's him or you. Now decide."

Seconds ticked by. The old mayor spoke. "They will kill you, son. And I am an old man."

This statement seemed to anger the captain. He slapped Carlos in the face and yelled, "I ain't gonna wait all day, you chicken-shit bastard. Now make up your mind!"

Carlos looked at the mayor through wet eyes. He knew that he couldn't harm this regal old man. And yet Carlos was only twenty-eight years of age. The last thing he wanted to do was die in a strange town so far from home. The last thing he wanted was to amuse a gang of bad men with his death.

Then Carlos had an idea. It was an idea that would prove him to be either the most cowardly man who ever lived or the craziest. *Most likely*, he thought, *I am both*.

He lowered the gun, took aim, and fired.

Chapter Three

Carlos awoke in a strange room. He looked around. There was a chair, a washbasin, a bedside table, and a wooden closet in the corner. And, of course, the bed in which he lay. He was covered with a thin cotton blanket. The room's only other feature was a small window covered by a white gauze curtain. It glowed with sunlight, and Carlos guessed that it had to be some time in the afternoon.

His foot throbbed with pain. He looked down and saw that the blanket had been pulled back at one corner to reveal his left foot. It was so wrapped with bandages that it was the size of a wasps' nest. In that moment, Carlos remembered the rebels, the old mayor, the town of Rosita, a pistol shot ringing in his ears. His mouth was dry, and his face burned with shame. He could still hear the rebels, laughing and pointing and saying, "He shot his own damn self in the foot!"

Carlos took a deep breath. His sadness lifted a bit when a second thought came to him. *Now I can go home. Now I will see my father and my little town in the South.* He pulled back the cotton blanket and sat up. Yet when he tried to stand, his foot throbbed as hot as the white part of a flame. He howled and fell back onto the bed, his skin now damp with sweat. Wave after wave of fresh pain flowed through his foot, reaching as far up as his knee. He tried to breathe away the torment, and failed.

Just then, the door to his room opened. A young woman poked her head in and looked at him for a second. Carlos was still trying to breathe away his pain when she left, closing the door behind her.

He lay back and stared sadly at the ceiling. He was still breathing hard. His hair, wet with sweat, stuck to his forehead.

A short while later, there was a light knock on the door. Weakly, he said, "Come in."

Three men and a woman entered the little room. One man was the old mayor, and the second was dressed in a priest's robe. A middle-aged woman wearing a silk gown and smoking a cigar in a long, black holder stood beside them. The fourth visitor was dressed in a blazer and riding trousers, like a rich Spanish landowner. He took a step toward the bed. The soles of his tall leather boots smacked the floor.

"My name is Antonio Garcia," he said. "I would like to shake your hand."

Carlos weakly reached out. "Carlos Orozco."

"I hope you have slept well. A woman in town... she gave you something to help you rest."

Carlos realized that his foot wasn't the only part of him that hurt. With every breath, his ribs howled. His hands were swollen, and he felt a sting in his lower lip. The pain brought back a little more of what had happened, like a moving picture shown on a screen before his eyes. After seeing what Carlos had done, the captain had attacked him, kicking him with his pointy snakeskin boots. If Carlos had not rolled into a ball, protecting his head with his big hands, the captain might have killed him.

"I hurt all over."

"I don't doubt it," said Antonio. "What you did yesterday was the noblest thing I have ever seen. They were going to kill our mayor."

"No," Carlos groaned. "I acted shamefully. I shot myself in the foot."

"Well, it worked," said the man dressed like a priest.

"Oh," said Antonio. "Let me introduce Father Alvarez. He is our priest. And this is Madame Felix. She is Rosita's most important… er… business woman."

"Hello," said Madame Felix. "After beating the living shit out of you, the rebels grew tired with our little town and rode off."

"They rode off?"

"With my girls hiding in every root cellar in town, I think they decided they'd have more fun elsewhere," she explained.

Carlos didn't respond, as the last piece of yesterday's puzzle was falling into place. When the captain had grown tired of kicking

Carlos, he'd stood there panting, his hands on his knees. One of the others had said, "You want me to put a bullet in his head, boss?" The captain spat and shook his head. "Oh no," he'd grunted. "I want this chicken-shit to live with what he did for the rest of his life."

Carlos heard Antonio's voice. "And I believe you've met Señor Cruz?"

"Do you remember me?" asked the old mayor with a smile.

Carlos ignored the question. Instead he looked at his four visitors, all of whom seemed pleased to be at his bedside. His eyes and his head now hurt as well.

"Whose house is this?"

"It is mine," said the mayor. "It is the least I could do. I am staying with Antonio until you are better."

There was a pause. Carlos glanced at his foot.

"Who fixed up my foot?"

"The same woman who gave you some sleeping medicine." Antonio said. "She is good at such things. You will meet her later."

"Now, don't you worry," added Father Alvarez. "You will remain here until you're better. Women from the village will cook your meals. There's also a girl who will keep an eye on you. She'll make sure you have all that you need."

Carlos felt tired. His entire body cried for sleep. "How long will I be here?" he asked.

The four looked at one another. Madame Felix answered. "Please, just relax and lie back. If you can do this, I promise that time will pass much faster."

After they left, Carlos slept. His dreams were alive with gunfire and sorrow and the pain of his beating. Some time later, the creak of the door startled him awake.

The village girl was stepping into the room. She carried a tray with a bowl of soup and some bread. She put the tray on the bedside table and smiled shyly at him, showing a row of white, even teeth. She had long, black hair and eyes as big as plums. Looking at her, Carlos felt a little homesick. She was short and wide-shouldered, like so many of the women of the South. Carlos guessed that she was about eighteen years of age.

She turned to leave.

"Wait," he said. "What is your name?"

She stopped, and turned slightly. "Linda," she answered in a soft voice. She then nodded and went out the door.

Carlos sat up with a groan. When he took hold of his spoon, his hand trembled, and pain shot through him. The soup was hot and tasted of chilies and lime. Night air cooled the room. He ate, feeling as alone as he'd ever felt in his life.

The next morning, pain awoke him from a deep, tossing dream. He sat straight up and fought to catch his breath. He felt as though lightning was shooting through his foot.

"Linda!" he called, his voice strained.

The girl rushed into the room.

"Please," he begged. "Help me."

She blinked twice and fled. About ten minutes later, she returned with an old, bent-over woman who smelled like kerosene. The woman was no taller than five feet and carried a large bundle on her back. Whiskers grew from her chin, and one of her eyes was so milky she had to look at Carlos sideways.

"Who are you?" Carlos moaned.

"They call me many things around here," she answered. "But the name's Azula. How's the foot?"

"Not good."

"Don't smell so good, neither. How's the rest of you?"

"Nothing compared to the foot. Please… can you help?"

"Don't worry. Probably just some bad spirits. They get stuck together and cause pain. Lucky for you I wasn't busy. I'll have you feeling better in a minute."

With a grunt, the old woman lowered her sack to the floor. Fishing around, she pulled out a glass bottle about the size of a deck of cards. The bottle was half-filled with clear liquid. She took out the tiny cork and moved toward Carlos.

"Now, I'm gonna put this under your nose. When I say 'go,' you sniff."

She wiped the tip of the bottle on her filthy skirt and placed it inside his right nostril. "Go," she said.

Carlos sniffed sharply. A river of poison flowed into his lungs and up into his brain. He coughed and turned blue. A second after that, the room turned soft, as if it were filled with jelly. He swore he could hear music playing somewhere in the distance. He watched the pain in his foot turn into a pale green cloud and float out the door. But the best thing? The shame he felt for shooting himself slipped away. He felt as if it had never been there.

"What was in… uh…"

"Extracts," answered the old woman. "Herbs mostly. A cactus stem or two. Maybe some mashed beetles. All mixed with a little ether."

Carlos felt himself floating out of his body, settling somewhere near the ceiling. He rolled over and looked down. As he watched, the old woman took the bandages off his foot. She reached into her bag and pulled out a clay pot. After prying off the lid, she scooped dark green slime onto Carlos's foot while rocking back and forth. To Carlos, whose back was still against the ceiling, it looked as though the old woman had gone into a trance.

When his foot was covered in goo, she reached into her bag and pulled out a bunch of dried twigs. She lit them with a match and shuffled around the room while chanting in a low voice. The air filled with the scent of burnt almonds.

After a few minutes, she stopped. Again, she reached into her bag. This time, she pulled out a small brush and a pot filled with orange powder. She brushed this onto the top of Carlos's foot.

Just as she began to remove the green mud, Carlos found himself being pulled back into his body.

"There," she said with a grin. "All better. Your ribs and lip will take care of themselves. Your mood is up to you. Now get some rest."

Chapter Four

Three days passed. Mostly, Carlos slept. On the fourth morning, he awoke with a strange feeling. Though his head pounded and his ribs still hurt with each breath, the pain in his foot seemed to be gone. Gently, he moved his foot from side to side, something that would have caused him to scream before. He sat up and pulled his legs around. Though moving still hurt, he could now picture the day when he would be better. With that thought, a moment of intense fear passed through him. He had come so, so close to dying. He had come so close to not *being*.

"Linda," he called.

The village girl came running. He paused for a moment, looking at her. "Tell me something," he said. "Why are you all being so nice to me here?"

She tilted her head and grinned. A dimple formed on each cheek. She shrugged her shoulders.

"Please," he said. "Tell me."

Without looking at him, she said, "You made the bad men go away."

Carlos cheered silently. It was her accent. She really *was* from the South. "They went away on their own," he said. "I had nothing to do with it. It was chance and nothing more. And by the way, call me Carlos."

She nodded.

"Oh, and one other thing. I think my foot's a bit better."

Later, Linda came back with a tall, thin man carrying a tape measure. He had an Adam's apple the size of an egg.

"Hello," he said.

"Hello," said Carlos.

"My name is Ramon. I am a wood worker."

"I am…"

"Please," he said. "I know who you are. Now, if I could ask you to stand…"

He helped Carlos to his good foot, and measured the distance between the ground and Carlos's armpits. He then left, but returned a few hours later. Smiling, he handed Carlos a pair of roughly made crutches.

"Thank you," Carlos said. "Thank you so much."

Ramon nodded, backed out the door, and was gone.

As soon as Ramon left, Carlos stood and slipped his crutches under his arms. He gasped and fell back onto the bed, holding the spots where his crutches had touched his cracked ribs. For a moment, he just lay there, staring at the ceiling and feeling sorry for himself. When he tried the crutches again, he found a way to hold them so they didn't rub against his sides. He walked around the room a few times, but soon both his ribs and his foot began to hurt. He had to return to bed.

Every few hours, driven mostly by boredom, Carlos got up and used his crutches a little more. The next day, he figured out how to use them without hurting his ribs. It involved a lot of hopping and leaning to one side, but he didn't mind. He opened the door of his room. For the first time, Carlos saw the front room of the old mayor's house. As in most homes, a hammock was strung between two support posts. A table, two chairs, and a mirror took up one wall. The front door was painted blue. The shutters over the window facing the street were closed. It was as simple as the front room of his own little home in the South.

Carlos moved toward the door and pushed it. It swung open with a creak. He took a step into the dusty street and looked from left to right. It was late afternoon, and the town was just coming alive after its midday rest. He could hear the voices of children and the barking of dogs. He was about to make his way toward the town square when Linda came running up. She looked flushed and upset.

"Carlos!" she cried out. "You should be in…"

"I'm okay," he told her. "Being outside is helping."

She glanced at his wrapped foot.

"Really, I am," he added. "With these crutches, I'm just fine. In fact, I want to see some of this town of yours. Why don't you show me a little of it?"

"Me?"

"Why not?"

"I am only supposed to…"

"Take care of me, yes? Well, right now I need a little fresh air. It wouldn't help things if I got lost, would it?"

She blinked. Her black eyes sparkled. During moments like these, her beauty leapt at him, as if coming from some place where wars were unknown.

"Then it's settled. You lead the way."

"All right," she said.

They began walking along the street in front of the mayor's house. Linda moved slowly, allowing Carlos to keep up. As they walked, he noticed how the sunlight reflected off her hair, making it shine violet. After a minute or two, they reached the plaza. It was full of people, all talking. As Carlos looked on, he thought of his own little town down south. There, the streets filled in the late afternoon and stayed full until well after dinner.

Just then, Carlos was spotted by the priest and the rich Spanish landowner. They both came over.

"Carlos!" said Antonio. "What are you doing out of bed?"

"It's the crutches," said Father Alvarez. "They're working like a charm!"

Antonio looked at Linda. "I think we can take him from here."

Linda nodded and turned. As she hurried away, Carlos looked over his shoulder and watched her for a moment.

"Come, come," they said. "Let us show you our little town. Really, it's so good to see you out of bed."

They took a slow, halting walk around the small plaza. In the sunlight, the pale adobe buildings were the same colour as the earth from which they were made. First, the friends showed Carlos the town hall, where the mayor had his office. Then, they showed him the village church, built by the Spanish six hundred years earlier. "It's still standing," said Antonio. "Say what you will, but we Spanish people know how to build things that last." They passed the hairdresser's and the place where an old man ground coffee and corn for a few pesos. They passed the town's only store, where people bought fruit, meat, and milk.

They reached the southwest corner of the square.

"How is your foot holding up?" asked Father Alvarez.

"To tell the truth, it's starting to hurt a little. My side as well. Though they weren't hurt as badly, I think these damn ribs are going to take longer to heal than my foot."

"You wouldn't happen to be a little thirsty, would you?"

"As a matter of fact, I am."

"In that case, there's a man who would like to meet you."

Carlos smiled. They were steps from the town tavern, which looked slightly charred from the fire. He followed the two men through swinging doors. The room was dark, small, and filled with five or six rough wood tables. The smell of smoke still hung in the air. The man cleaning glasses behind the bar turned and beamed at them. As he stepped out from behind the bar,

Carlos noticed that his arm was wrapped in a large bandage.

"Welcome," he said. "Please. Sit. My name is Fernando. Whatever you want… it's on the house."

"Really, you don't have to treat me."

"It's the least I can do," he said. "Please…"

Carlos worked himself into a chair. Resting his wounded foot felt good. Fernando rushed off and came back with four beers. He sat and joined them. After a few sips, he said, "You know, while they were in my tavern the rebels were talking about coming back that night. Can you believe it?"

Fernando looked up. Carlos did, too, and saw that the ceiling was a mess of splinters and bullet holes.

"And then, when I dared to suggest they pay their bill, they poured tequila on a table top and lit a match. The tequila burst into flames, and that was the fire you saw. Of course, the fire was easy to put out, but I burned my arm. And *still* they were saying they'd be back for more."

"It's this damn war," said Antonio. "It has lost all meaning. Each side has been taken over by killers and thieves. It's all about money now. The people who sell guns and bullets won't let it stop. I suppose all wars are that way."

"Of course," said the priest. "Of course."

Fernando looked at Carlos. "Either way, you did me a great favour, Carlos Orozco."

There it was again. This stupid idea that somehow Carlos's actions had caused the rebels to leave. His face reddened, and he felt angry. He had shot himself in the foot. It was the action of a coward. He was just about to explain this when church bells started ringing, even though it was not the top of the hour. The four men all looked in the direction of the street. Antonio rose, and pushed open the tavern doors. Sunlight speared the gloom and travelled to the rear wall of the bar. Dust hung in the air.

Carlos watched as Antonio stopped a middle-aged woman who was racing past the door.

"What's happening?" he called to her.

"Haven't you heard?" she yelled back. "It's the mayor!"

Chapter Five

————

Shortly after Carlos awoke the next day, he heard a slight knocking at the door of his room. The sun had already reached the highest point in the sky.

"Just a minute," he called.

He struggled to his feet and opened the door. Linda was standing there, holding a suit of clothing.

"Linda," he said with a smile.

"You've missed the funeral Mass," she told him. "But they haven't buried him yet. Hurry."

She passed Carlos the suit. He thanked her, and watched as she left the house. As he dressed, he thought about the old mayor. Even though he was eighty-two years old, he had gone hunting for deer in the hot, noon-hour sun. An hour later, his horse had trotted back into town without a rider. Its arrival had sparked fear in the townsfolk who loved him: had he met a band of rebels or army soldiers? A few men armed themselves as best they could and went looking. After an hour or two, they found the old man lying on the desert floor. He was staring straight up at the sky, not a mark on him, his rifle still in his hands.

The suit fit Carlos well, though it was a little loose around the waist and hips. He wondered who it had belonged to. He slipped on a belt and put some tonic on his dark hair before combing it. He then looked at himself in the mirror. It was the first time he had done so since his injury. Now that his body was on the mend, he was eating well. He enjoyed taking showers that flowed from the rainwater tank perched on top of the house. Even his bottom lip had healed, though it still looked a little puffy and blue. As he looked at his image, he tried to decide what sort of person was looking back.

He went outside, where Linda was waiting for him.

"Wait," she said. "Wait here."

She turned and hurried off. A few minutes later, a peasant chewing a length of straw came by in a cart pulled by a burro.

"Antonio sent me," the peasant said. "This is his cart. The funeral is out of town, at the old mission church. The mayor liked to go there to watch sunsets. He'll be happy there."

Carlos slowly climbed on board. Just as he turned to see whether Linda might be coming with them, the driver clicked his tongue against his teeth. The burro pulled away, the wagon bouncing on the bumpy street.

At the central plaza, they took a lane running south into the desert. The ground grew stony, and the cart started rocking from side to side. Carlos grabbed the seat on either side of him, but the peasant swayed from side to side, giving in to the motion. The cart went up a little hill, toward an old, crumbling church.

They stopped. The sun was straight above, burning white-hot. A blanket of dust hung in the air, too lazy to float back to earth. The townspeople had gathered around a freshly dug grave. Carlos got out of the cart and thanked the driver. He limped toward the crowd and saw that the casket had already been lowered into the ground. He spotted Antonio, Fernando, and Madame Felix. They, in turn, nodded toward him. A few women were crying. Otherwise, no one made a sound.

After a few minutes, Carlos heard footsteps. He turned and saw Father Alvarez walking toward them all. His robes swung as he walked, and his bald head gleamed in the sunlight. He had a prayer book in one hand.

He stopped at the edge of the grave.

"We are here today to say goodbye to one of our most cherished sons," Father Alvarez said. "A man who did his job with love in his heart and pride in his step. A man who loved children, though he never had any of his own. A man who helped those in need, a man who went to church every Sunday. A man who would do anything to protect this town of his, who was simple and brave and just. A man we were proud to call our mayor."

As he spoke, Carlos thought of how the old man had stood up to the rebels. He asked himself if a man could be brave without being at least a little bit stupid. Maybe, he realized, this was the nature of courage. It wasn't just one thing, but a mixture of many things. Maybe courage was a thing both good *and* bad.

When the service was over, the cart driver met Carlos outside the churchyard. Just as they were about to pull away, Antonio came up.

"Carlos," he said. "Father Alvarez and I are going to the tavern. Do you want to come?"

"Of course," he said.

"Then meet us there."

The driver clicked his tongue against his teeth. His burro lifted his tail and farted, as if to say, "It's hot out. I want to rest in the shade." Then he slowly started for home. After a few minutes, Carlos turned to the cart driver.

"Do you know Linda?" he asked.

"Linda? There are many Lindas in this town. It is a well-used name, yes?"

"The one looking after me."

"Oh yes. *That* Linda. The Indian girl. Yes, I think I do."

Carlos paused. "Take me to her house."

"What do you mean?"

"Take me to her house," Carlos repeated.

"But why?"

"I want to see where she lives."

"I don't think you'll like it," said the driver.

"Why not?"

"I just don't think you will."

"I don't care."

The driver shrugged his shoulders and said, "Okay."

They went along a rocky trail until it reached a T. Instead of turning toward town, the driver turned right. Carlos knew where they were headed. Just east of town was a camp. He had heard it spoken of many times. They rode for a few more minutes, and then came over a ridge. Carlos saw a cluster of shacks built from scraps of wood and tin.

As they neared, Carlos wrinkled his nose. The driver saw this and said, "Some of their kind need a good bath, if you ask me."

Carlos ignored the comment, though the camp did smell of smoke and horse sweat and milk left too long in the sun. All around were low fires, fed by dried animal dung. Little children played in the dusty lanes, wearing nothing but dirty shorts. Skinny, flea-bitten dogs followed along, hoping for scraps.

The cart stopped in front of a tilting tin-roofed shack. Peering inside, Carlos could see women in long skirts. A man slept in a hammock.

"This is it," said the driver. "She lives with an aunt who came from the South a long while ago, I believe."

"All right," said Carlos, his body feeling heavy.

"Do you want…"

"No. Let's just go."

The driver clicked his tongue, urging the burro forward. As they rode back to town, Carlos thought of all the ways in which God chose to treat his children. If there was a good reason for any of it, he would really like to know.

Carlos grunted his thanks when they reached the tavern. It had been a long afternoon, and his foot was throbbing. He also felt that he could use a drink.

He pushed open the tavern door, letting light wash over the room. The door closed behind him, and the room returned to a cool gloom. He spotted Antonio, Father Alvarez, and Fernando and sat with them.

Antonio lifted a shot glass. "To the mayor," he said.

"To the mayor," they all replied.

They drank and then slammed the bottoms of their glasses on the table top.

"So," said Antonio. "What do you think happened to our old friend? Do you think rebels hiding in the desert shot at him?"

"He didn't have any bullet wounds."

"Maybe he fell trying to get away."

"He *was* eighty-two," said Father Alvarez. "Could be he had a heart attack."

"Why was a bullet missing, then?"

"Maybe he took a shot at a deer and missed."

"That would be my guess," said Antonio. "You all know how clumsy Roberto could be."

They all chuckled and drank another shot. As the liquor loosened their tongues, they started sharing memories of the old man with Carlos.

"Remember the time he fell off his own roof trying to install a rain spout?" asked Antonio.

"Or," Fernando added, "how about the time he stepped outside this very tavern and spooked Madame's horse? He got himself kicked in the chest!"

"How about the Sunday morning when he tripped in the church aisle?" said the priest. "Remember how he smacked his head against a pew? How the sound echoed off the walls of the church?"

"Yes! Yes!" said Antonio, laughing. "And then he jumped back up, saying he'd just been looking for something that had dropped from his pocket."

"And meanwhile," said Father Alvarez, "blood was rushing from the cut in his forehead!"

"I tell you," said Fernando, "it's lucky that old man lasted as long as he did."

They all laughed except Carlos. The others noticed, and there was a guilty silence. Though Carlos's heart had lightened a little when he entered the tavern, the strong drink had brought back his dark mood. He couldn't stop thinking about the way that Linda lived, way out in that filthy Indian camp.

Antonio broke the silence.

"So," he said. "I guess we need a new mayor."

Chapter Six

———

Carlos's foot was healing, and his ribs didn't complain as long as he didn't take a deep breath. Instead of crutches, he now used a cane that Ramon, the wood worker, had made for him. He got into the habit of walking slowly through the town most days, resting on a bench when he got tired.

One morning he awoke and decided to peel away the strips of cloth binding his wound. It was the first time he'd taken a close look at what was left of his foot. Each time the old woman named Azula had tended to him, he'd turned his head. He refused to see what he'd done to himself. This time, though, he just stared. The three smallest toes were gone, leaving tiny, bruised stumps.

About half of the second toe was gone as well, leaving only the big toe without any damage. The entire foot had turned various shades of green and yellow. Carlos lay back, feeling awful.

That afternoon, when Linda brought him his midday meal, he asked if she would like to eat with him.

She paused at the door. She was looking down. "I don't think I can," she said.

"Why not? It would save me from eating all by myself."

She remained standing at the door, saying nothing. Her body swayed slightly, and the light caught her blouse. He noticed the outline of her small, compact body moving against the fabric.

"Linda," Carlos said. "Please."

She nodded, and filled two metal plates with a spicy rabbit stew. They sat at the table, steam rising into their faces. As they ate, Carlos found that the food began to lose its taste. The gentle way she held her spoon, the careful way she pushed her hair away from her face, distracted him. He was lost in the plumpness of her mouth.

"Linda," he finally said. "May I ask you a question?"

She nodded.

"It's just that... you're from the South, yes? Like me?"

"Yes," she whispered.

"Why are you living here?"

She stared at her food.

"It's all right," he said. "I shouldn't have asked."

"No... it's... We were farmers. The rebels came."

"I'm sorry."

"They told us we had to give them corn or they would shoot us," she told him.

"So you gave them corn."

"Two weeks later, the army came, asking for corn as well."

"Which you didn't have," Carlos said.

She sniffled. "Of course not. When they saw that our grain bins were empty, they said we must have given it all to the rebels. They said we must have been *helping* the rebels. I was fourteen, and like all the other girls, I was hiding on the outskirts of the village."

Carlos didn't need to hear the rest of the story. Linda was telling him about the day she'd lost her family.

Just then, someone knocked at the front door. Linda jumped up and answered. There stood Antonio and Father Alvarez, with Madame Felix standing in front of them. She wore a dress that looked like it had been shipped all the way from France. As always, she was smoking a narrow cigar in a long, black holder.

Antonio looked at Linda, at Carlos, and at the two bowls of stew on the table. He seemed confused, as if his mind couldn't understand what his eyes were showing him.

Linda saw this. She rushed over to the table, dumped the food on her plate back into the pot, and took her plate into the kitchen. A moment later, she moved past Carlos's guests, bowing her head a little before leaving.

"She is a nice girl," said Madame Felix. "Too bad they aren't all like that."

"Yes," said Father Alvarez. "A real gem. It's a pity how her life turned out."

Carlos looked around the room for places for them all to sit. He began to stand. "I'm sorry..."

"Please," said Antonio. "Stay seated. You've got the bad foot."

Carlos did so. Madame Felix took the other seat. Blue smoke drifted from the tip of her cigar.

"Can I get you something?" asked Carlos. "I think there might be some fruit juice out back."

"No, no, thank you very much," said Antonio.

Antonio and the priest exchanged glances.

"Well, we might as well tell you straight out," said Alvarez. "The three of us talked things over till three o'clock this morning. We have given this much thought."

Again, they paused. It was Antonio who spoke next.

"Carlos," he said, "we would like you to be our new mayor."

"Me?" The idea shocked Carlos.

"Yes. We have all talked about it."

"But why would you want *me* to be your mayor?"

"You have a thoughtful, gentle manner," Antonio answered. "That's something this poor country of ours could use more of. As well..."

He glanced at the others, and cleared his throat. "As well, you were given a problem that could not be solved, and you found a way to solve it. Better yet, you did it without killing or being killed. You have qualities that few of us possess. You set an example not just for this town, but for the whole of Mexico. If everyone was like you, we'd get through this damn war with our souls clean."

Carlos shook his head. "I shot myself in the foot. I am a coward. All I want to do is go home. Nothing more."

"Carlos," said Antonio. "You see ways around problems instead of through them."

Carlos looked at his three visitors, still thinking they were not serious. "The only thing I want," he said, "is to get better. And then I want to go home."

The next day, when Linda brought him his midday meal, she smiled.

"What is it?" he asked.

She put down the small pot she'd brought him and lifted the lid. Carlos couldn't believe it. The women of the village had cooked him chicken in a sauce made from chilies and bitter chocolate. It was a wonderful dish from his state in the South.

The women had also made him real corn tortillas, instead of the flour tortillas that they ate in the North.

"Please," he said. "Tell them I am grateful."

Linda left before he had the chance to offer her some. He sat at his table, eating. The meal wasn't half bad, although he could teach them a few tricks about making the rich sauces of his home state.

A few hours later, with the taste of his meal still in his mouth, Carlos heard someone at the front of the house. He limped to the door and opened it. There stood Father Alvarez.

"Good afternoon," said Father Alvarez.

"Good afternoon," said Carlos.

"I have something for you," said the priest. He held a small statue of a dark-skinned Virgin Mary. It was just like the one people prayed to in Carlos's home state. The priest put the statue on the floor next to the hammock. "I thought you might like this," he said. "I know they have entire festivals for her down south..."

The two shared a long, awkward moment. Carlos looked at the floor.

"What?" said the priest. "What is it?"

"Please," said Carlos. "I know what you are trying to do. I know what you are *all* trying to do. But really, my mind is made up. I'm not going to be your mayor."

"As you wish," said Father Alvarez. "We are only trying to make you happy during your stay here."

The priest bowed, and then left. Carlos sat down and started to brood. His foot had all but healed. Indoors, he even walked without his cane, though his foot still ached if he did it too much. Yet he lost his balance often because of his missing toes. He would have to learn to walk all over again.

Carlos had another problem, too. If he left for home, he knew that one of three things would happen. One, he could reach his village unharmed. Two, he could be caught by the rebels, who would either shoot him or force him to fight on their side. Three, he would be caught by the Mexican army, who would either shoot him or force him to fight on their side. Trying to go home would be very risky. His foot would have to be perfect. He would need more time.

One week led into another. His balance improved. Each day, Carlos found he could walk a little farther without pain coming to his foot. Then, even when it did come, it wasn't the sharp stabbing that it had been. Instead, his pain became more of a bother than a curse. Soon he would be ready.

On Saturday nights, a band always set up in the central square and played the awful polka music that people liked in the North. Carlos had been in Rosita for five weeks, and each Saturday he had listened from his bed. The music made his foot and ribs ache. This week, he would go. No matter how much he disliked the music, he did like the people of the town. He was feeling bored and restless, and a little fun would do him some good.

Around seven o'clock, just as the skies began to turn orange, he dressed in the suit he'd been given for the mayor's burial. He then limped to the plaza, leaving his cane at the house. Almost all of the townspeople were there. Children ran in circles and men passed bottles and women chatted. In the middle of it all, a deer was roasting on a spit, a look of surprise frozen on its face. Around eight o'clock, when the deer was cooked through, slices were cut off and served with lime juice and beans.

Around nine o'clock, with the smiles of the people lit by torch light, the musicians headed to the bandstand. They began tuning their guitars and horns—a process which sounded, at least to Carlos, like a pig being killed. Carlos began to tell people he was sorry, but he had to leave. His foot was starting to really hurt, and he needed his rest.

Just then the band started playing its first song. Carlos couldn't believe it. This wasn't polka music. It was the music of the southern states. It was the music of the singers known as "mariachis." He could tell that the players were not used to this type of music. But he could also tell that they were trying their hardest. All around him, people started dancing. Carlos even danced himself. When his foot started to hurt, he still wouldn't sit down. Instead, he kept most of his weight on his good foot, so he began to look as though he was hopping.

He looked around, hoping to spot Linda. She simply wasn't there. At one point, Antonio caught him scanning the crowd.

"Looking for someone?" he asked.

"No."

Antonio's face darkened. He cleared his throat. "Listen, Carlos. The Indians… they don't often come to these little parties of ours. It's not that they're not welcome. It's not that at all. Oh no. It's more that… well… it's more that they prefer their own kind, you see?"

Carlos nodded. His face had reddened, and he hoped that Antonio could not tell in the low light. Antonio walked off, whistling.

A few minutes later, Carlos ran into Madame Felix. Though it was her busiest night of the week, she'd decided to take a break.

"Well, hello, Carlos," she said.

"Madame."

"What's this I hear about you still not wanting to be this town's mayor?"

"Madame, I don't want to be *any* town's mayor. I'm a cook. That's all."

Madame Felix looked at him oddly. "You know what I think?"

"What is that, Madame Felix?"

"I think maybe you don't know *who* you are."

"You could be right."

"Well, I have news for you," she said slyly. "In this world, any problem can be fixed."

Carlos stayed for a few more beers, along with a plate of deer meat and refried beans. When his foot was so sore he could barely place it on the ground, he limped home. He put himself to bed, angry that maybe he had overdone it.

He was just starting to drift off to sleep when he heard a knock on the door. Thinking some drunkards were playing a trick on him, he didn't get up. The knocking went on. Carlos swore. He rose and hopped to the door in his night shirt.

A young woman stood in the doorway. Carlos swallowed. Her skin shone like the skin of an olive. Her lips were the colour of a plum. Her figure was as curvy as a mountain road. And her eyes! They were the eyes of the night, of mischief.

She held up her right hand. In it, she carried a sponge.

"Hello," she said.

"Uh, hello," said Carlos.

"I am Maria."

"Maria?"

"Yes. I work for Madame. She is the one who sent me. I have come to give you your bath."

"You are going to give me a… bath?"

"Oh yes," she said, smiling. "I was told that you are very, very *dirty*."

Chapter Seven

Carlos awoke the next morning alone. His head pounded. His mouth felt dry. For the first time since he'd come to this little town, he ached in a place that was not his foot or ribs.

He dressed and limped along the lane leading to Antonio's big house. He knocked on the door. A minute or so passed. Carlos knocked again.

Antonio answered. His hair was uncombed, and his night shirt was rumpled. When he saw Carlos, he broke into a huge smile.

"I take it that you have given a second thought to being our mayor?"

Carlos looked down. He felt like a bad guest.

"Antonio," he said. "I am so grateful for all you have done for me. For *all* the town has done for me. But when I woke up this morning, I knew that I could not stay here any longer. I woke up to the smell of perfume on my pillow. I knew that by staying here I was giving you all a false hope. The truth is that I will not be your mayor. I am not fit to be any town's mayor. I am going to return to the South and tend to my cooking pots. It is the only thing I want."

The smile left Antonio's face. When he spoke, his voice was no longer cheerful. "You do know that the war is still raging hard?"

"I do."

"And you are ready for this? I have heard awful stories."

Carlos agreed. "I have heard them as well."

The two looked at each other. Carlos knew that he would miss Antonio. He would also miss Father Alvarez and Fernando and Madame Felix and the rest of the town's kind people.

"Carlos," he said. "I own a horse and buggy. Tonight, if you want, we will travel under starlight to the town of Saltillo. It's best that way. I have heard that the trains are running off and on. If you wait long enough, you might find one that will take you to the capital. If the train isn't raided by rebels, army soldiers, or bandits, you might even get there. From there on, you'll have to take your chances."

"Thank you, Antonio Garcia."

"Meet me here at eight o'clock. And I promise you, no one will ask you to be mayor again."

Carlos nodded his head in thanks. He left, and made his way back through town. He stopped at the front door of Madame Felix's brothel. He knocked, and waited. Madame herself opened.

"Carlos!" she said. "How was your evening?"

"I came to thank you, Madame. Maria showed me that I could still feel joy. She showed me I could still be happy as a man."

"I knew she would."

"I have also come here to say goodbye. I am leaving tonight."

Madame looked at him in the same way that Antonio had. "Well, you can't say we didn't try. Goodbye, Carlos Orozco. You are a fine young man, and I believe you would have made a good mayor. People like you don't come around every day."

Next, Carlos visited the house of Father Alvarez. The priest had just finished shaving, and still had flecks of soap on his cheeks. Upon finding Carlos at his door, he grabbed a towel and wiped his face.

"You are leaving," he said.

"Yes. I am sorry."

"No need to be sorry, my son. God has given you free will. We only tried to help you decide how to use it."

"Father, I was hoping that you could help me with something."

"What is it?"

"I have a long trip ahead of me. Many dangers are out there. You know this. I was hoping you could give me a blessing."

Father Alvarez nodded and stepped into his house. When he came back to the door he held a small, clear bottle. He pulled out the cork and splashed a little holy water on Carlos as he said a prayer.

"Goodbye, Carlos Orozco. I will never forget the day you came to us. I will never forget what you did that day."

"Neither will I," said Carlos. Without warning, his eyes started to redden. "I wish I could not say that. But it's true. I will never forget that day either."

Carlos then made a stop at the tavern. There, Fernando thanked him, yet again, for saving his bar. He poured them each a drink.

"To the lovely torment that is Mexico," he said.

"May she live forever," added Carlos.

Then Carlos left. With a pain forming where his missing toes had been, he walked east of the town. The sun burned down on his neck. His foot started to throb, and he began to worry about his trip back to the South.

When at last he entered the Indian camp, all heads turned. Children stopped playing tag, and dogs stopped digging through garbage.

He found Linda standing in the doorway of her hut. A small pig was rooting at her feet. She kicked it and it ran off, squealing.

Carlos walked up close to her. She smelled of lime and wood smoke and a scent that was hers and hers alone. She wore a loose white cotton blouse that fell from her shoulders. It covered a part of her body that made Carlos think of good things only.

"You are going?" she asked.

"Yes. I have to. This is not my home."

A tear formed in one of her big eyes. It broke free and rolled down her cheek. Carlos stood looking at it, as though it was some sort of marvel. A rainbow, perhaps. Or snow on a distant mountain.

"I am not crying over what I want," she said. "I am crying because if you go back to the South, what happened to my parents might happen to you. I am crying because I will lie awake each night, praying you haven't been killed."

Carlos then did something he'd been longing to do since the moment he first saw Linda. He touched her, his fingers brushing her face. They turned damp with the salt of her tears. Her wet eyes reached into him, torching his soul.

When they kissed, a breeze kicked up from the east, whipping her hair against the side of his hot, hot face.

Chapter Eight

As planned, Carlos knocked on Antonio's door at eight o'clock. But, to Antonio's surprise, Carlos did not have a suitcase with him.

"What would I have to do?" asked Carlos.

Antonio grinned.

"Not a lot," he said. "Be nice to people. Sign papers sometimes. Keep the peace. Shoot the odd stray dog."

"There doesn't seem to be a lot of crime here."

"There isn't any at all."

"Would I be paid?"

"Once in a while, a cheque will come from the state government. Not often, but once in a while. But as long as the war is on, the cheques won't be any good anyway."

There was a long, long pause.

"Antonio Garcia. Do you really want a coward to be your mayor? Do you really want that for your town?"

"If you are what a coward is, Carlos Orozco, then my answer is yes."

The next day, Carlos visited the mayor's office. It was upstairs in the town hall, the two-storey adobe building on the square that his friends had shown him. He liked the office's view over the north end of the plaza. The padded chair that came with the job looked nice, too. He could imagine greeting people in this cool, shabby room, his desire to help them as real as the sun was round.

That afternoon, Carlos went to the tavern. He did the same the next day, and the day after that as well. After a couple of weeks, he stopped correcting people when they called him Mayor. His foot healed for good, though he was left with a slight limp. He knew that limp would stay with him for the rest of his life.

The war ended, and his thoughts slowed to match the pace of the town. Before very long, he and Linda got married, blessed by Father Alvarez. Every couple of years, he visited his father in the South, though he noticed that he missed his new home in the North. Linda felt the same way, so they mostly stayed close to home. He and Linda had children, and Carlos loved them with the strength of a madman. Carlos read a lot, and he hunted deer with the other men. Afterwards, in the middle of the desert, the hunters would eat smoked meat and rice boiled in stock and bay leaves.

Carlos also learned to spend hours thinking of nothing at all. With this talent came an ease with life that he had not had before. One day stretched into the next. He made close friends. He fell in love with the sight of a sunset over reaches of sand. Studying the dull, grey desert birds, he came to see their beauty. He even grew to like polka music and the food of the North. Decades passed. As he grew older, he learned that, at times, joy could be so sharp that it felt almost painful.

When Carlos was eighty-three, Linda passed to the next world. Their six children, who all lived in the United States, came for the funeral.

His four girls stayed for a few weeks. The oldest, Margarita, was the last to leave. When he finally convinced her that he would be fine, he walked with her to Rosita's new bus station. She kissed him and said, "I love you, Papa." She rode off waving, a fifty-two-year-old woman who was the spitting image of her mother. She even had a grandchild of her own.

"Well," Carlos thought as he waved, "it won't be long now."

The sickness came right away. Within months, he spent more time asleep than awake. Once again, the village cared for him, hiring a young girl to bring him soup and bread and fresh towels. At times he became confused and began talking to her as though the year was 1920, and her name was Linda. The girl did not correct him. She preferred to say, "Yes, Carlos, war is an awful thing. Now, eat your soup. It is getting cold."

One day he came awake with a clear head. He knew that it was to be his last day alive. He did not feel sad. For the most part he had been a lucky man. He had also been wise enough to enjoy his good fortune. This ability, he knew, was not enjoyed by most men. Women perhaps, but not men.

Carlos prayed that day, looking over at his little statue of the Virgin Mary. He remembered when Father Alvarez had brought it to him all those years ago. He wondered how long it had been since he'd had a drink with Father Alvarez or Antonio or Fernando. With a shock, he realized that they had all been gone for more than twenty years. Yet he could still picture them as clearly as if they were right there beside him. It was funny, he thought, how memory worked. It could put you in many different places, all at the same time. Like most things in life, memory was a sort of magic.

He closed his eyes. In his head, he said goodbye to each of his children. They were all in their forties and fifties. Still, he could remember how their baby skin smelled whenever he lifted one of them from a rainwater bath. He was careful to say how much he loved the thing that made each of them different. He also told them that he understood their need to have a better life in America, even if he had died a little bit every time one of them left.

He then moved on to Linda. He told her how much he still adored her and that he would see her soon in heaven. Now that this silly thing called life was over, they could be side by side forever. One day, they would be with their children as well.

"Don't worry, my darling," he told Linda. "This short time that we've been apart will soon seem like it never even happened."

Yet when his final moment came, Carlos thought of the same thing he'd thought about each day of his life in Rosita. He thought of the day the rebels came to town. But this time, with death looking him straight in the eyes, he felt no fear. This pleased him. He was a brave man, after all. He was no coward, after all. He laughed. It was so funny—he'd fretted about something untrue for so long. He then enjoyed his final breath and stepped toward something light-filled and unknown.

Good Reads

Discover Canada's Bestselling Authors with Good Reads Books

Good Reads authors have a special talent—
the ability to tell a great story, using clear language.

Good Reads books are ideal for people

✳ on the go, who want a short read;
✳ who want to experience the joy of reading;
✳ who want to get into the reading habit.

To find out more, please visit
www.GoodReadsBooks.com

The Good Reads project is sponsored by
ABC Life Literacy Canada.

The project is funded in part by the Government of Canada's
Office of Literacy and Essential Skills.

Libraries and literacy and education markets
order from Grass Roots Press.

Bookstores and other retail outlets order from HarperCollins Canada.

Good Reads Series

If you enjoyed this Good Reads book,
you can find more at your local library or bookstore.

✳

The Stalker by Gail Anderson-Dargatz

In From the Cold by Deborah Ellis

New Year's Eve by Marina Endicott

Home Invasion by Joy Fielding

Picture This by Anthony Hyde

Missing by Frances Itani

Shipwreck by Maureen Jennings

The Picture of Nobody by Rabindranath Maharaj

The Hangman by Louise Penny

Easy Money by Gail Vaz-Oxlade

✳

For more information on Good Reads,
visit **www.GoodReadsBooks.com**

Home Invasion
By Joy Fielding

Kathy Brown suddenly wakes up. Was that a noise in the house, or part of her dream?

In her dream, Kathy was about to kiss Michael, her high school boyfriend. Her husband, Jack, lies beside her, snoring. Michael is exciting. Jack is boring.

When Kathy hears the noise again, she gets up. Then she hears whispers. Then she feels a gun at her head. Two men are in the house. Kathy and her husband face a living nightmare. Kathy must also face her real feelings about her husband.

The outcome surprises everyone, most of all Kathy herself.

About the Author

 Robert Hough knew he wanted to be a writer when he was still in high school. He is the author of three bestselling novels. His first book, *The Final Confession of Mabel Stark*, was translated into fifteen languages. Robert lives in Toronto with his wife and two daughters.

Also by Robert Hough:

The Final Confession of Mabel Stark
The Stowaway
The Culprits

*

You can visit Robert's website at
www.roberthough.ca